For Thomas and Oliver—FW
For Helen, Evan, William, Gen and Sara—AY

Published by Allen & Unwin in 2019

Allen & Unwin
83 Alexander Street
Crows Nest NSW 2065
Australia
Phone: (61 2) 8425 0100
Email: info@allenandunwin.com
Web: www.allenandunwin.com

A catalogue record for this book is available from the National Library of Australia
catalogue.nla.gov.au

ISBN 978 1 76029 094 8

For teaching resources, explore www.allenandunwin.com/resources/for-teachers

Cover and internal design by Julia Eim
Set in 11 pt Conduit ITC Light by Julia Eim
This book was printed in November 2018 by C&C Offset Printing Co. Ltd, China.

10 9 8 7 6 5 4 3 2 1
www.franceswatts.com

MY FRIEND
FRED

Frances Watts

illustrated by A. Yi

ALLEN & UNWIN

SYDNEY · MELBOURNE · AUCKLAND · LONDON

My friend FRED eats dog food for breakfast.

I think dog food is disgusting.

My friend **FRED** loves
to chase balls.

He never gets bored.

My friend FRED sniffs trees.

I'd rather climb them.

My friend **FRED** gets excited
when the doorbell rings.

He can be very noisy.

My friend **FRED** wears
a coat when it's cold.

He thinks he looks handsome.

I'm not so sure.

My friend **FRED** digs holes.

He knows he shouldn't.

My friend FRED
doesn't like stairs.

Stairs are easy for me.

My friend **FRED** shakes himself after a bath.

I **hate** baths.

My friend **FRED** howls
at the moon.

I don't know why.

My friend **FRED** always turns around
three times before he goes to sleep.

2

3

He does a lot of funny things.

But even though we are different,

FRED is my best friend.

Frances Watts is an award-winning author of more than 25 books for children. Her first picture book, *Kisses for Daddy*, illustrated by David Legge, was a CBCA Honour Book and has been published in 20 languages. Her next book with David Legge, *Parsley Rabbit's Book about Books*, was a CBCA Book of the Year and *Goodnight, Mice!*, illustrated by Judy Watson, won the Prime Minister's Literary Award. Frances lives in Sydney, Australia.

A. Yi is an illustrator and animation artist. She has illustrated various children's books, including *Ivanhoe Swift Left Home at Six*, written by Jane Godwin, and the best-selling Alice Miranda series, written by Jacqueline Harvey. She likes doodling and wishes all books were illustrated.